First published by Albert Street Books, an imprint of Allen & Unwin, in 2023

Copyright © Text, Sophy Williams 2023
Copyright © Illustrations, Gavin Scott 2023

All rights reserved. No part of this book may be reproduced or transmitted in any form or by any means, electronic or mechanical, including photocopying, recording or by any information storage and retrieval system, without prior permission in writing from the publisher. The Australian *Copyright Act 1968* (the Act) allows a maximum of one chapter or ten per cent of this book, whichever is the greater, to be photocopied by any educational institution for its educational purposes provided that the educational institution (or body that administers it) has given a remuneration notice to the Copyright Agency (Australia) under the Act.

Allen & Unwin
Cammeraygal Country
83 Alexander Street
Crows Nest NSW 2065
Australia
Phone: (61 2) 8425 0100
Email: info@allenandunwin.com
Web: www.allenandunwin.com

Allen & Unwin acknowledges the Traditional Owners of the Country on which we live and work.
We pay our respects to all Aboriginal and Torres Strait Islander Elders, past and present.

A catalogue record for this book is available from the National Library of Australia

ISBN 978 1 76118 026 2

For teaching resources, explore www.allenandunwin.com/resources/for-teachers

Cover and text design by Kirby Armstrong
Set in 23 pt Times New Roman by Kirby Armstrong

This book was printed in March 2023 by C&C Offset Printing Co. Ltd, China

10 9 8 7 6 5 4 3 2 1

Feelings are WILD

Sophy Williams · Gavin Scott

ALBERT STREET
BOOKS

One koala feels **grumpy.**
His naptime was too short.

Two bunnies feel **nervous.**
What if they get caught?

Three lion cubs feel **restless.**
Time to have a walk.

Four crocs feel **frustrated.**
They've just run out of chalk!

Five possums feel **sad.**
That branch is hard to climb.

Six piglets feel **ashamed.**
They fell into the slime.

Seven mice feel **shy.**
They won't come out for dinner.

Eight penguins feel **worried.**
Their snowman's getting thinner.

Nine kittens feel **afraid.**
There's a puppy dog next door.

HOME 130
AWAY 129

Ten quokkas feel **excited**.
Check out that final score!

Now it's time to count back down and check in on our friends.

Nine kittens feel **surprised**. The puppy's made amends.

Eight penguins feel **reassured**, but still a little **glum.**

Seven mice feel **brave** and **bold**
and eat up every crumb.

Six piglets are feeling **proud.**
They've scrubbed up such a treat.

Five possums feel **happy** now. They have lots and lots to eat.

Four crocs feel **cheerful.**
They're playing with a ball.

Three lion cubs feel **peaceful**.
The night begins to fall.

Two bunnies feel **relieved.**
They only got a warning.